Raising Kids in the New World Order

A conservative approach to raising children; yours, your family's, and your neighbors'

J Holland

Holland & Holland Publishing

Copyright © 2020 J Holland

All rights reserved

The characters and events portrayed in this book are fictitious. Any similarity to real persons, living or dead, is coincidental and not intended by the author.

No part of this book may be reproduced without express written permission of the publisher.

Printed in the (hopefully still) United States of America.

Introduction

This book is intentionally printed in a larger print for the easiest of reading for all of us, as we are still waiting for our assigned bureaucratic eye appointment, or we have finally given up.

Children are kids and kids are little people, with undeveloped brains. Children think they are bigger, or older, than they really are. Often, even as they grow, they will tell you they are bigger, but their physical size maintains the truth.

Children may originate as a fruition of love. Some children may come as an accident of your love assembly, but never told. Nonetheless, all children are here and now your responsibility, so *they* say…

Accidents are not always bad, like the time I accidentally added lemon mint in my soup mix which turned out wonderfully and super tasty. Some of you may now wish you had added lemon mint or an alternative spice instead of the baby batter.

Children are a blessing even though they can cause depression and *grey* hair. Children can be as extraordinarily different as the words *grey* and *gray*.

Just like the varied spelling, children are diverse copies of their parents. Some kids are equipped differently and assuredly could appear to be angels, or indisputably act like the demon-possessed.

Although I would love to discuss some of the latest and most troubling disparities of modern children, I must remain conscientious in my pursuit to help all of us raise kids in the coming New World Order.

Some of our children are being taught to spy on their parents, friends, and neighbors, or at least, turn them in for any infraction of the law. Invoke parental control by forcing your children to denounce their policing and join the forces of the family unit, or suffer eradication from this earth, or twisted ears.

My mother always said that she brought me into this world, and confidently could take me out, although she never tested this theory in its fullness.

Even a dog can raise pups, but is that good enough, or should it be? My mother said a bunch of things and as my mother always said, "You can't make a dog cook your breakfast, when you stay in bed all day. And it surely won't get the laundry done!"

I am not sure if my mother attempted to actually teach our dog to cook, but I think she might have tried. Just thinking that maybe this is why our dog was always trying to taste foods that we left lying around. Come to think of it, maybe she tried to teach the neighbor's cat to cook, over at their house.

The world is changing very rapidly, as the river of advancement flows by, whether wanted or not. Our children will need to learn from us, which will allow them to live and gift us with grandchildren. Grandchildren bring extra love and laughter that were not offered by your children, or mine.

Grandchildren are a blessing, if you are permitted to spend time with them. These grandchildren also increase your chances of being scammed by the filth that call pretending to be your descendants, while begging for money. By learning more about your kids and grandkids, you lessen your own chances of getting scammed, by criminals. …not your kids.

This book is not about politics because the progressives, the coup, and the *chinese* government control that part of your life. This book is a preemptive strike to raising your kids correctly and keeping them alive and helping, on your team.

Children sometimes are not all yours, and sometimes just show up in your basement. Many children, if not most, do have friends. Occasionally children are in your home because of other children or simply for the free food, snacks and ~~beer~~.

It is illegal to allow a child to drink and you assuredly want to set a good example by putting your mask on, staying indoors, and being a good citizen by pretending to fear the wrath and allowances of the overlords and czars. When the governmental home occupation count shrinks, be a good parent and vote the heaviest child off the island.   ...or is it the unhealthiest? ...or shortest? ...or puny?

Maybe it is time for the wee-wee'd people like us to stand up as 'We the People' and raise another great generation of kids, or at least better than ours.

In honesty, these children will be the same offspring that will be changing our diapers, giving us our stack of mandatory medications, and checking our vitals to see if we are still alive. I don't want my kids to scream into the hallways of the adult prisons, "I got another almost dead one. Get me a cart and a new sheet! Hey, I might need a club this time…"

Credits & Ideas

Editor and consultant – JMHolland & Barbara

Cover Photo – *Image by* lisa runnels *from* Pixabay

Special Thanks – My Anomalous Family

1st book in this series – **Eating in the New World Order**

This author has other books available on tough subjects using an allegorical formula within a story.

For links to the first book

(KAKO HellCniht, A Demon Speaks)

www.HellCniht.com

or Search for J Holland on Amazon

Second Book – Coming Soon(ish)

KAKO HellCniht, Bound for Gehenna

Contents

If you don't like to read 10

A Real Education? 12

Clothing & Media 15

Children & Books (Shh…) 18

Kids & Drinking 20

Social Skill Building 22

Children Come Preprogrammed 24

Some Issues are Edible 28

For Pete's Sake 31

No-Fault Spanking 32

Something's Up There! 37

Absorption 38

Restroom Thoughts… 40

Good Relationships 43

Fires in the Wind 45

Time's Up! 46

Dedication Page 49

Afterword 50

If you don't like to read

And…

A Real Education?

This question has become a money-making proposition in the last century and across the globe. What makes the certificate of one college more prestigious than another, with requirements that are all issued from the same basket of necessities, and by the same governmental agency? It is either a sneaky secret, or an enigma of mass magnitudes.

There are many accredited and countless nonaccredited degrees. If you have spent a barrel full of money getting an unrecognized degree, then you have, and sadly so, failed to work the system that the government has built for your benefit.

Some degrees are easy and valueless to obtain, and soon all kids will need to obtain one in order to work at the local burger-flipping joint, that is a prime management position trainer. The best concept about the greasy spoons of the past, was that people truly cared about your food. Now, the employees are concerned in securing any excessive paycheck and less concerned with the customers, or customer care.

Another coming bliss will be that your child's concrete education, offered to anyone, at the cost of the taxpayer(s), is prized among the elites, like everyone else with a free education. But think, with higher wages coming, as maximum minimum wage takes hold, everyone is again a big bloated winner.

If you can spell degree and have the paperwork to prove it, why not offer a starting salary of $20/hour. But wait, there's more… In best application of minimum wage, skip the chump change and offer at least $50 or $100 per hour. Seems silly now, since my cheeseburger will cost $102 dollars soon, but remember that your kid, and mine, are smarter and will be shrewder than the average bear, right?

At first read, some of you may have thought that I had a long introduction to this book, and I appreciate your judgements. Although I don't agree with them, I have elected to believe that you have feelings and ideas, and will not however, censor my words like most of the social media, whether you use it or not.

Any education, or your child's education, should be trustworthy and truly support their needs and keep them alive. The rest is all foo-foo on paper (fu-fu.)

Math is a great skill if you need to cook for more than one person and are keen to follow recipes. It also gives kids advantages when calculating sizes of containers and drums for supplies. Furthermore, it predicts proper trajectories of solids if needed, both small and large, whether fired, tossed or launched.

Reading is a must. Teaching children to read, and to read proficiently, will give them an undisputed advantage in general society, penal circles, or reeducation centers. Reading books, of old and new, will build an internal appreciation that cannot be beaten out of them. History will enable your children to see the needed drive to salvage the past, and bring a halt to destroying the present, and maybe attention to the future. Reading can be a good thing.

Writing is a skill that all children should learn and learn well. You are a parent and the tutor in any area of writing. Please instruct the child with real letters, real words, and real terminology. To acknowledge phrases and slang is acceptable, but to repeat and write them, is not necessary. Why repeat phrases of stupidity and barbaric formation, or accept this as pure normalcy? Don't offset progress with folly.

Clothing & Media

Children have tendencies to want more expensive clothing as they get older, until they literally price you out of possible purchases. The younger the child, the easier that child is to purchase for. Some clothing to include shirts, pants, and shoes, can be hand-me-downs. This passed-along clothing is not only cost-effective, but good for the environment, if you still believe in Santa Claus, or overpopulation.

Your used infant clothing can be passed to other friends and family members, and can be traded like stocks on the market. Good pieces come with minimal stains and a reminder that bibs work. Some foods such as green peas, orange squash and red beets will undermine any clothing trading program.

The media, cartoons, family shows, sitcoms and more, have been subverted by evilness. With every new episode, the typical cartoon gets a new character from the gender confusion group, or the current character catches the irrelevant-dad syndrome. Sometimes, the fond and cherished cartoon goes on an overstuffed mindbender about causes that are years above any child's true understanding, or care.

I am not happy with the incessant direction of which we should be more concerned with animals and fish, and less concerned with a baby. Some in our society, possibly even in your inner circles, have been convinced that it is better to assign a death sentence, than to allow the actual birth of babies. Even thinking like this is disruptive to natural thoughts, and so, I rest my case in saying, "Babies rock and in their ignorance, they truly need you!"

To fight God is a losing battle, whether you believe or not. Maybe it is best said, "God rocks and, in my stupidity, I truly need Him!" Even my acquaintances know that a picture can be sent by snail mail, but rather wish to be brainwashed by using mind-altering apps, or programs of censorship. In their defense, they say that they are smarter than the average bear.

Growing up in Penn's woods, I knew a few bears and they were not using any social networks, but still managed to find me, every time...

My clothes during these bear encounters skipped the tradeable piles, for sure. Did you know that a bear is more afraid of you, than you are of it? I am not sure that this is true, because I never read a single story of a human attacking a bear and then eating it.

Does anyone find it odd that we want to dress our kids in clothes, produced in countries all over the world, but not ours? What happened to being excited about dressing your child in an American-made shirt? I am sure that if my parents could have picked up a good used flag, with conviction they would have dressed me in it, from underwear to coat.

I do know you can't use the flag for dress. As our children learn to be less American, they become such. As our children learn to accept iniquity, they build a foundation of debauchery. Ouch! Teach a child to light a fire, build bridges, and host an honest party, but don't teach them to burn a building, yell at the officers, and poop in the streets. Your child is a replica of you and your values, standards, religious affiliations, morals, ethics, beliefs and more.

Do you know what social stream your kid is fishing in, or the bike path upon which your child is racing toward the finish? Not every checkered flag is for a winner or even the correct race, now is it?

Children & Books (Shh…)

Children say outlandish things, truly. Some of the things they say are funny, cute, and very innocent. Sometimes they say things that should not ever be expressed in words. Sometimes they even say things they do not understand. Other times, things are said by them that should never be talked about, ever, by anyone. But still, children say outlandish things.

Some children need to improve a little and others a lot. Improvement is a tough word with far too many opinions. Let's leave the opinions to the experts and review what we know to be tried and true principles, that have elfin, or at least small, disputes either way.

But then again, books of all sizes can be great tools for mind development and critical thinking.

Books – General Warnings:

- Most books are being eliminated because they do not fit the evolving agenda, or deception.
- Caution: Some books can promote thinking outside the mainstream, and that is "OK!"

Be wary of telling others about your books. They, others you may know, might stop being your friendly friends. Trusted friends are rare and only the reliable few should be allowed to share your reading secrets. Life and death clashes have been caused by books, as reported in historical writings, now being burned.

If you are puzzled in finding a good book, consider talking to an older reader and requesting their perspective. When still in doubt, talk to a few of the oldest people in your neighborhood about books. They might surprise you with vast knowledge, and a variety of options. …quietly for everyone's sake.

If you hide actual books outside, you might best seal them with a '*gamesaver*.' If you do not know what a 'gamesaver' is, this book was a gift to you, rather than an actual survival guide to raising your children.

If you seal a book by other means, a few silica packs, saved from previous online purchases, are necessary. Quart sized or gallon bags are vital to keeping the pages pristine(ish.) Moisture can ruin readability.

If people question the hole digging, remember this phrase, "Darn dog died and I can't just eat him, because he was my friend and deserves better!"

Kids & Drinking

Children are too young to drink, even in our changing world. If we were in a European country, our kids might not only enjoy a glass of wine, but be permitted to grab us a beer without fear of government intervention, or apprehension.

Alcohol consumption in children has been studied and the reports show that drinking excessively might stunt physical and mental growth. Other studies show this identical effect in grown adults. Although a drunkard might think they are taller, bulkier, and tougher, they are not. They are however less likely to suffer serious injury as they fall easily, and often.

Children are kids and give the impression of little-minded people trapped inside a perplexing body that is rapidly changing. A child's mind is adjusting, and at times, seemingly, too much or too little.

In a duly responsible way, my mother often told me that it was necessary, every now and then, to prop my brains up when they settled into the bottom of my rear. She would always alert my father when this problem needed correcting, and he would oblige.

Although she was able to correct this problem when it was needed, I assumed that she wanted to include the entire family, or at least let my father be justly involved. Drinking as a child might have made this a more bearable activity. However, finding alcohol as a child was impossible in my home.

My parents did not drink alcohol in any considerable amounts, although many in my larger family did. Some of my extended family used it to preserve their organs in order to live longer, in a pickling fashion. Most of them are still preserved today, walking and talking; granted their speech is slurred on occasion, but their vocal cords are aged like a fine red wine.

I have noticed that some parents in my inner circles have, at times, given a sip of this, or that, to their child. My only honest worry is that not all friends are true friends, and this might complicate things.

Experts call excessive drinking an illness. It's one of the few diseases in which you willingly bring it to your lips in a cup and partake of it, this bad sickness.

Social Skill Building

Children are bombarded with far too much garbage today. The garbage has been piling up in our televisions, social circles, and outdoors for a long time; so, the cup *runneth* over. A child does get the brunt of the trash and mostly, we adults are permitting it and at times, encouraging it.

The televisions are no longer pillars of education filled with moral teaching, but an indoctrination center of lies, deception, and stuff that wasn't allowed to even be printed in the magazines of old. And you might ask of others, or yourselves, why?

Unfortunately, children are like sponges and will absorb bad social behaviors which can be squeezed out into society, upon their friends, or even yours. Children cannot adapt socially to the world, unless we are mingling with them and teaching them to couple or conjoin to the world in a helpful custom.

Allowing children to learn socially acceptable behaviors on their own, or as they see presented everywhere, is like asking for a stick of dynamite to be placed in a freshly plucked hotdog bun and smothered in a plethora of colorful condiments.

Sure, you won't remember much after the first bite, but the impact of your presence will be flying around everywhere, for a very, very long time.

Delight in teaching children old skills that once made kids fun, respectable, and loving. Teach a child, any child you meet, to act with a sense of courtesy, coupled with joy. There are enough unhappy kids bouncing around in society, spreading sadness, that simply need a good spanking, or at least our help in some positive or reinforcing manner.

"Thank you!" and "Please!" could add a proper and civil beginning to your child's terminology and favor their acceptance in the *new* and upcoming world.

Effective communication is a virtuous thing for any child. A child should not necessarily be afraid of you, but nonetheless, still remember who the parent is, at all times. Parents should not be afraid to break any bonds between a child, and connected children, who are permitting and promoting unhealthy skills, or inherently building creepy social activities.

Children Come Preprogrammed

Kids are not mindful or innately generous from birth, and so there are traits and manners that need to be taught by us, their parents. It is a fact, long forgotten, that children will do things that please themselves, and less to please us, save we introduce them to the subject of sharing, caring, and love.

I don't remember a single child, when wanting or needing their mother, put forward a request, by saying, "Please, might I suckle?" and assuredly it will never happen. Infants are self-centered and brilliantly able to scream incessantly about a need. Identifying the specific need of any fussing child is the problem and they know it, as well everyone else.

Teach growing children to focus on creating decent and positive interactions. Teach them by setting a good example, watching programs with good examples, or even better, reading a book about such.

Sincere communication is a must, now and in the near future, for any child. Dishonest communication will result in poor applications in life; low paying jobs, last place in the food lines, and additional prison time beyond the required stint for any other conservative, or Christian parents and their kids.

There is an order of events and a hierarchy of people, which should be correctly taught to your children. These mere kids should not be placed on the top, but rather on the last rung of the stepping ladder in choices and decisions, relative to their maturity.

Kids answer to parents, who answer to their bosses, billing companies, and interact cordially with friends and acquaintances, authorities, and older people. If this system becomes unbalanced, the system perishes like any society that prides itself on communal concepts like transformation, socialism and marxism. Should I capitalize on concepts that won't work, ever? Two reasons to not capitalize, aye?

Exceptions to these simple rules do make for a very messy ending. Omissions of one or two branches of this tree of knowledge create more destruction than an oiled-up stripper would, while wildly swinging on a pole in your living room, kitchen, or bathroom.

If this is not understood, seek added insight from your parents. Children need to learn that it is good for them to finish school, get a job, earn a living, get married, have children, and so on. These are the steps that allow them to keep moving onward and upward. These are steps that keep them flourishing.

A child might need to learn in a more rapid style, assuredly quicker than normal, if certain stages of life are skipped. If the baby comes before marriage, or school, or other steps are simply rushed, life obviously still continues, but your assistance is expanded, along with your financial obligations.

It is not normal for a child to expect the best because they are merely there and possess a fabricated and futile faith that they are much deserving, before they even leave their isolation chamber in your basement.

Most preprogramming that comes gift-wrapped inside the child's little mind, will need to be pulled out over the course of their precise upbringing. Occasionally much pulling is needed and other times simple coaching and coaxing works miraculously.

Children are smaller than normal adults, but as they grow, their brains do not seem to obtain much size compared to the intake of food. During the teenage years, their brains actually disengage only to recouple and rejoin later in life, say in their late 20s.

Some of us might question the disconnect of neurons, or the scientific study that proves such happenings, however, our world is full of evidence, and proof can be ultimately visualized in any family setting. Loose wires inside of children can be verified methodically, technically, and scientifically.

Nearly all preprogramming is different in each child. Each kid comes with a greater or lesser degree of this here programming. Nevertheless, it is very rare to find a child that is in need of minimal repair, but if so, you might best buy a lottery ticket, as you are rather lucky. Heck, maybe buy two or three.

At times, some children might sound like their codes have been hacked and they are now being operated by a foreign agency. Even so, if this is truly the case, this child is under an internal reset, that is easily dealt with by added rest, extensive lecturing or a good old fashion reminder, with or without force.

It is possible to reprogram children effectively, and successfully create a helpful and positive member for your family. Who knows, they might even go on to become a productive member of society. Surely you have noticed that a bunch of codes are out in society of an unbreakable nature, because these children are running amuck, destroying things that they will soon need to repair, and be paid for by your taxes. Should we tell them, or let them destructively roam?

Some Issues are Edible

Kids range in size and shape. Some kids are skinny, some are fit, and some are fat. Before you, the reader, become upset with the word *fat*, let's reiterate my meaning with a better explanation. Fat is not considered a substance applied to the exterior of a child before cooking, whether derived from excess oil of an animal or a vegetable. Too much fat is not a question of cooking, but a state of overall size. Not all fat should be treated the same.

Although much attention may be showered on the skinny kids, the fat children need substantial assistance, also. It is not uncommon to spend genuine time investigating why a child is overweight rather than just enjoying the festive plumpness that comes with a holiday season, the Christmas season!

Let's be honest, a skinny kid also might have issues, but assuredly will not break your furniture. It may take good effort to determine the true cause of uncharacteristic and unexpected growth. Furniture is expensive, so obesity is well worth investigation.

If you, as a parent, are also overly sized and the blame cannot be pushed to at least one of the thousands of excuses offered, you might need to stop dishin' out such large amounts of the government cheeses, picked up in those big ol' food lines.

We honestly have failed children by allowing them to eat as they please, and whatever they please. To correct this, we, the parents, will need to suggest to them, if by stimulus or force, a good eating plan, which can be adopted by us. Children can eat a ton of food, but shouldn't eat this ton in one sitting.

Eating too much food causes a child's body to work harder and create extra hormones and enzymes. Children already have an abundance of chemicals naturally disrupting their apparent sanity, without intentionally adding more. Extra acid secretion adds excessive reactions during digestion, which produces burping and farting. Gases should be kept to a manageable level and leaks should not be recorded.

Kids have been given brains and a body that need good foods for ripening. Healthy foods to eat are greens, nuts, fruits, vegetables, fish, oats, peanut butter, eggs, and similarly related items. Products like tofu and lentils are not very tasty or *cookable* or even eatable, unless you work for a schooling system, food agencies, or you fib about them, a lot.

Cookable is not a word, but it should be. It clearly describes savory things, and not things like soy, broccoli, or zucchini. However, these bad things can be cooked correctly with cheese to provide broccoli cheesy bread, zucchini cheesy sandwiches or veggie covered nachos. Every child loves cheese and cheese will make uncookables, …cookable.

Sadly, there are kids that are cheese-intolerant. These children are easily identified as they are isolated, tucked in a corner, or sitting on a bench watching the other children eat cheese. Allow them to blend in with normal cheese-eaters by providing them with a cheese looking substitute such as a sweet potato sauce, imitation cheese spreads, vegan spreadable imitation twaddle, or cashew cheese.

Even though there are alternatives, notice that they all identify with the seductive word "cheese" or look like real cheese. In addition to this cheesy lotto wins for all, does anyone know how to milk a cashew, or any other nut for Pete's sake?

For Pete's Sake

Well, for the 'love of Pete' and definitely for the 'sake of Pete' we should adhere to the best advice of our government authorities and educated leaders.

Another peculiar question, in a time where we are not allowed to question anything, is, "Who got us into this mess?" …rhetorical questions are allowed?

I would like to know who this Pete character is. Any ideas? …and thirdly, why are we listening to a guy named Pete who lists zero credentials and is vastly unknown? Why not listen to unrestricted ideas of people with rather distinguished names like Walter, Clifton, Jim, Sir Isaac Flapperstien, or even Joe.

Let me elaborate on the *'Joe'* name. I was referring to the identity of an actual wise and perceptive person who could construct four, mostly real English words, which might be easily discernable, into a sentence in such a fashion that would be translated into sense, better wisdom or knowledge of any sort. Someone like Joe Schmoe.

No-Fault Spanking

Spanking is a word that offends some people, and only excites a few. Spanking could identify a good time, like "Hello darling, I had a spanking good time last night!" It could also indicate a bad time, like "Hello doll, last night was just spankingly awful!" However, it is usually indicative of actual spanking.

Spanking usually includes two parties; one issuing the spanking and the other, receiving. In our New World Order, the government could, can, and will institute instructional plans on types of spanking permitted, and some with oversight, I am sure.

Some state governments have already issued laws regarding the spanking of a child, whether your own child or another in the neighborhood. These arbitrary orders were written by uninformed people that do not clearly understand the concept of spanking, or paddling, or properly rebuking a child.

Even when searching for credible and positive effects of paddling, all sources are now pointing to negative subjects or worse and much gloomier suggestions that shouldn't ever be mentioned, again.

Spanking is not a sport, nor an exercise that should be conducted lightly. In the good book, Proverbs 22:15 lists a dutiful requirement in opposition to the current indoctrination or schooling. "Foolishness is bound in the heart of a child, but the rod of correction shall drive it far from him."

Proverbs 23:14 registers the simple concept as such, "Punish them with the rod and save them from death." This sounds like a lifesaver…

For those not keen on Biblical understanding and would rather believe expert advice coming from research, experience, or statistical evaluation only performed in a timed, catalogued, and documented study, should note that no faithfully linked negative effects to kids were ever reported to those who were spanked less than once or twice a month. Even caregivers' research has cataloged positive effects of spanking, in good and respectable fashion, of course.

In our refutation of *their* truth, it is extremely difficult to do honest research online without being bombarded with an almost unsurpassable mound of their selected data, because they simply say that you cannot "handle the truth," and you "are too dumb."

But if I dare be frank, there are many resources that instruct proper discipline of children up to, and including, the physical spanking of a child, as needed, and when needed. These instances are often found in the isles of big-box grocery markets.

To spank a child to promote joy for yourself, or provide relief from your anger, are not good motives, or morally acceptable. Spanking a child to provide an added reminder to choose a more appropriate path or action in the near future, is a morally acceptable endeavor, and stands strongly with good parenting.

Many in the world today will suggest, and have suggested, that spanking does not work or that they have found easier or less severe alternatives. Easy for whom is the better question; the parent or child?

Deciding for yourself is difficult and you might need to consult your parents, or your grandparents, on this specific subject. Spanking did work for me. Spanking probably worked for you. If you bought this book, you have a job, which is proof that spanking is a positive and wholesome thing.

They, the elitists that know better than you, say that spanking causes mental health problems, reduced thought processing, and self-esteem issues. What if *they* are wrong and the Proverbs are right? What if *they* are trying to pull the proverbial mask over your eyes and just possibly, God knows best? …wool?

As an added bonus of positive persuasion to assist in unsurpassed applications of correction, I offer this. If you spank a child in front of their friends, the kid might decide to do better, in quicker fashion, to avoid the embarrassment, which will improve their overall mental health and self-esteem. It will always bring more honest and genuine relationships with your child's friends, whether they know it, or not.

Although they say spanking sends mixed messages, I was pretty sure it meant that the thing I did, was assuredly wrong. The only mixed message that I received, was in the item used to do the spanking.

In opposition to my opinion and to energize the reader with the authority's views and counseling, of whom many are not even elected but rather appointed by other non-elected bureaucrats, I have listed some of *their* alternatives, or better ideas.

- Time-Out: Provides time to prepare for more excitement or better excuses. *Yelled* in loud fashion to scare the child into submission.

- Losing Privileges: Doesn't all the stuff belong to the adults anyway? Did your kids come with stuff and if so, where is it? Ouch?

- Teaching Better Skills: Isn't that already our job? This should not be a surprise - is this not what the spanking is gifting the child with?

- Rewards: Don't children receive free rewards like food, water, shelter, and love?

- Consequences: Why can't spanking fit into this alternative? Isn't spanking a good, healthy, and just consequence of a negative activity?

- Praise: This is a given, always and forever in love. Kids seek praise and fewer spankings.

- Penalties: If I take money from the child, it was my money to begin with. If I spank a child, it would be considered a very strong, very direct, and extremely clear penalty, wouldn't it?

Something's Up There!

Some scholars might slam my reliance on God, or my thoughts of good versus evil. Regretfully, some readers might not like my word *evil* rather than *bad*.

Still, other readers might be angry about the mention of any mysterious force, beings or even bears. Some might even be irritated because I have found a higher power or a greater being than theirs. Some of you might even throw this book into the nearest dumpster because I didn't mention rebirth or regeneration, or even the plethora of gods that some love to follow.

Well, never fear, my words are here to help all of us in this New World Order by giving some insightful lines and instructions. God is there whether you want Him to be, or not. He has taken an interest in the little children and apparently has an agenda, regardless of your way, or your displeasure of Him.

There is nothing wrong with teaching good things. Somehow, for some reason, something or someone could go wrong, if *good* is the end of the lesson.

Absorption

Right now, most of the big-box networks work against our country and definitely against "We the People." They have begun an assault on us as individuals, us as parents, and our little absorbing children, who are being mentally assaulted.

These entities have openly stated that they have your, and my, best interest at heart by not allowing you to see or hear the truth. These nanny-bots redirect you to other *authoritative* sites and *networks* that repeat the filtered and alternative information, and call it truth – *real truth*.

Avowedly our children are caught in the middle, but we are promised a fair resolution. Our children spend massive time mimicking our behaviors, our actions, and our words. Kids are dry sponges waiting for a flood of solutions, whether nourishing or toxic.

Truly there are people that cannot handle the truth and we have specialized buildings without corners that you can periodically visit. If you cannot handle the truth, you need to do your best to not have children, or have those children in your care. Truth does matter and it is not outweighed by concocted facts, as one leading socialist randomly declared in a speech, that seemingly came from the clutches of a communistic oligarch or recesses of the underworld.

The word fact does have a definition and that definition should not change. In this forcefully confusing time, the elites are now magically changing definitions. Teach your children well. Teach them that words do matter, and definitions are truly concrete, truly solid, and truly long-lasting.

The texture and value of these word changes are equitable to the actual remnants of stuff left in the diapers of our children in their younger ages. It might be warm and fresh, but it is horribly scented and stains anything that comes in contact with it.

If you do already have children and are afraid of the truth or afraid to find truth, then please drop your children at your grandparents', because your parents have also failed you. Truth is not learned by kids, unless it is taught by adults, or those caring for the little ones. Truth is unchangeable, people are not.

Restroom Thoughts…

I recently had a friend tell me to make sure that I capitalize the word "We" and "People" in that overworked phrase, "We the People," and I began to wonder if that truly be the right application of capitalization. Confidently it is not a *woke* phrase, or even woke to capitalize the words that represent so many of our population. I am sure that many in our great country would prefer it to be removed from our vocabulary in its entirety, but I haven't and won't remove it. I am sure swarms still care about it.

The beacon of light which is shining upon the world is getting dimmer and dimmer. We are the People that rightly hold the *off&on* switch and need to keep it clutched tightly. Teach the children the way of truth and rightly place their little hands on the tops of ours, to keep the light bright as we get weaker.

I love the People that stand solidly for our country as the spiritual-warfare-forces pound heavily upon the outer and inner walls. I am saddened, however, with the people that have opened the doors to our country and let in the evilness that showers us with disappointment, almost daily, and relentlessly.

I love those great Americans who reflect the uprightness and the righteousness in "We" the "People", but I do not respect the capitalization for those that use the phrase "we the people" to mean progression of socialistic and dangerous ideologies.

To redirect, when I was small, my clothing and shoes were picked from a bin in a store that had many bins. Mounds of shoes and clothing were stuffed in a bin much taller than me, but tactically placed for an adult to assess. There was no screening of the shoes or clothing, other than what I could see above the rim of the bins, as they were planted in these types of stores, like a persistent chinese bombing campaign.

My father would reach in the bin, pull out a size of his choosing, and request me to put the item on my body. There was no need for any dressing rooms, because we were kids and most everything fit right over last year's clothing, clinging to our body, and purchased from the same steadfast store.

If it was a pair of shoes, my father would pull up my pantleg, force the back of my puny foot to the rear of the shoe and say, "Room to grow!" and toss them in the basket. If it was clothing, my father would twist and turn it on my body, and say, "Room to grow!" and toss these in the basket, as well. Now that I think about this adventure in the labyrinth of a jungle, as my father called it every year, maybe the store was called "Room to Grow."

In preparing for the coming uniforms and rags, worn hand-me-downs, and other shabby items that will be forced upon you, you might begin to practice the above "*room to grow*" concepts. At first, your child might whimper and cry, but with practice, these new image-desensitized children will be better prepared than most, and less willing to be singled out.

When the hammer falls, and the slice of moon glows in the nighttime sky above, even your child will thank you for the added help. Adjustments need be made now, to accommodate for fewer tears later, and besides, do you honestly think you are going to find tissues or toilet paper for added wiping, of tears?

Nighttime will be cold some months, and *room-to-grow* clothes might be a thankful treat to keeping the warmth around one's body.

Good Relationships

This is seemingly a mysterious question to almost all children, of any age. Firstly, we should describe the word good, from an adult standpoint, even though some children have some useful ideas. Secondly, we should describe the word relationship, as many children have some wild and crazy ideas about this.

Good as a word is rather valuable, if not overused. Most of our children are now more interested in doing things for the greater good, than actually being a good steward of the earth, for honorable reasons.

There is nothing wrong with being a good child, for goodness sake, but it should unremittingly have substance, or good reason. Kids should learn that being good, doing good, and wanting good for others is not just cliché, but an avenue to please others and especially their parents, and elders.

Good varies from being acceptable to exceptional. So, if I had my choice, I would not be that happy with a child who is just a winner, as these awards are freely given to all children today. More assuredly, I would be happier with an exceptionally good kid.

A relationship is a recognized union between two humans in such a fashion that it can be viewed in public, without embarrassment. Uhm…, well, from a child's perspective shall be our viewing point.

Children are able to involve adults and other children in their little circles of friendships, or relationships. Creepy old men, carrying signs about "lost puppies" are wicked people and should be annihilated from society. Furthermore, any adult that intimidates a child into arrangements that are inappropriate or otherwise deemed *adultish*, should be added to the list of hunted vermin, and removed from the general public permanently and as quickly as possible.

Bad friends are easy to find, if you have some money, and are willing to buy and share stuff. Good friends are willing to help you with your family and offer suggestions for raising your kids. Great friends are those who you trust changing your child's dirty diaper. Super splendid friends are those gifted with the opportunity, and willing to do it without asking.

Fires in the Wind

There is communication that gets us, *to* and *from*, in conversation and then there is conversation that carries the winds needed to stoke a fire.

Well, you only want a fire when a fire is needed. You surely don't want a fire when you can't find a bucket of water, or even a garden hose on full blast. To travel in words is a great delight, and the travel ways should have a start and a finish line for enjoyment, like a book with a beginning and an end.

Be honest, and teach children to be honest and trusting within virtuous reasoning. Children can't trust everyone, anymore, as some people just have bad intentions and bad ideas in their beastly heads.

Children are too innocent and need to grow with understanding and instruction from you; the adult, that parent, or the smarter neighbor on the block. Trusting any kid to a bunch of hoodlums is a bad mistake that none of us can afford in this everchanging and oversensitive time in the village.

Time's Up!

Thank you for enjoying the humor that I have put into words and hopefully you have found it a relief in these never-ending and troubling times. I appreciate the interest you have had and ask that if possible, stand for truth, and send a book to a friend.

I am an author and have published other words about our dilapidating societies, in a fun-filling(ish) read. I am working on a series and have found that no future conviction has honor in its own country, or state, or city. People find more excitement in online apps...?

In my first book in this series, **Eating in the New World Order**, I enlisted good fun and jokes, about our coming changes to America. Factually, I am not sure, and neither are you, of what actually happened in our 2020 Election. There are many pointing fingers to reasons and problems, and pointing fingers from one side to the other side, and many more pointing fingers with flashing signs that we are unable to draw correctly in this type of book.

I tried to be more serious in the wake of this coming storm of change and destruction to the country I love, but I am flabbergasted, dumbfounded, and rightly troubled that so many are willing to burn even the stores and neighborhoods they live in.

If we could just see the coming end of the world, or just the end of America, as we know it, we would gather all the tools needed to dig in and stop the theft of our great country, wouldn't we? Surely, and regardless our interaction, we will see change and continue to see change, in some better ways and in some worse ways. That is the nature of change, isn't it? Or should it be?

I typically am unable to win a bet, but would be willing to put a bottle of baby powder up for grabs for anyone that believes we are honestly making progress with the progressives.

Isn't that a flagrantly abused and oxymoronic word? Facts matter and people's freedom matters, or at least, I thought it used to. I would be willing to toss a clean nappy to any one of our officials that might need one, but then again, we would cause a shortage.

As I always say, and have picked up and carried close to my heart, in the shortest of learned phrases, "If it wasn't this, it would be something else." A wise man in his 80s spouted this in my direction for the last twenty years, and by golly, come Gehenna or high water, he was right again, as usual.

We live on earth and are unfortunately subjected to the laws of creation, deceptive laws of the elected and unelected officials, the coup, and the people that control the food lines. Right now, we are subject to communist penetration, but too many people can't see the ingredients of the cookie, even as it crumbles.

God's will and direction are the only sure thing, in this confusing time filled with craziness, masks, and rules implemented by a squad of mindless monkeys randomly pushing buttons. What is a bunch of monkeys even called, if I might dare ask?

Your kids are here and more will come. Shall we provide them with truth or falsity? Children lie enough without our help and surely, as the sun comes each and every morning, our children will continue to lie without any help in the future. We need to make corrections and revisions for the better.

Dedication Page

- ✓ To my wife for listening to me lament about America. She not only edits my work, but edits the needed portions of my life, and most importantly, believes in me. I am real, after all!

- ✓ To real American parents who truly want to overhaul the indoctrination of American kids. …and to those who raise children that will be truly kind when I end up in a nursing home.

- ✓ To my parents – better than most. They taught me that winners win and losers are always last.

- ✓ To Mr. Lantz – Seriously, someone needs to tell this guy, "Thank You!"

- ✓ To the chickens that bless me and the fresh ones, after a random dog eats the old ones.

- ✓ To my neighbors – we need to stay a TEAM!

- ✓ To my friends, of which I have very few. I swear I will help, as I can, when we are taken.

Afterword

Raising children is a difficult chore, like cooking, except with other ingredients. People who raise well-behaved children make me happy and are beneficial; both parents and kids. Parents should do the best job possible, regardless the tools that they are afforded. All parents should have friends or other parents to bounce ideas off of, and hopefully, you have found good ones; friends, and kids!

I can't get over the new cancel culture that is destroying our world. I can't comprehend the acceptableness of the new woke capitalists, either. They are selling us a drug that we will never be able to get enough of, and even so, they hold all the stash. Does anyone see the problem with that? ...anyone?

Please remember that if you have found a helping handful of parents to form a group, be careful to be vigilant in offering good opinions, as they are useful. If you have useless or questionable opinions, keep practicing your skills of logical deduction and critical thinking, and keep quiet and listen at first.

If you are unable to conquer your fears of raising children and your opinions are even questioned by your spouse, maybe consider bringing in an expert like your grandparents, or see if you are able to drop your children off at your grandparents', on a more permanent basis. Choose to do the right thing, now!

This book might find some companions in the future, such as *Common Sense in the New World Order,* and *Hiding in the New World Order.* My book, *Eating in the New World Order*, might also give you a laugh. Rubber band them together, and hide them!

My joy still comes from knowing Truth and I know that this is all I rightly need, as the good book says. The rest and most of all that we participate in, is merely extra money stuffed in a savings jar; some smaller, some stiffer and surely some not worth the recycled paper it was printed on.

I once knew a man who raised a good flock of kids at the edge of a city forest. Every one of the little kiddies were darling girls. I will leave you with his famous words and his last remark, "These little chicks haven't laid a single egg all year long. Margie, should we keep feeding them anyway?"

Made in the USA
Columbia, SC
31 March 2021